The Poop Fairy

Written by Lori Isaac
Illustrated by Carolyn Owen

To order additional copies of this book, contact:
Xlibris Corporation
1-888-795-4274
www.Xlibris.com
Orders@Xlibris.com

Dedicated to
my precious
grandchildren,
Todd, Grace and
Steven Wadding

Hello, boys and girls.
My name is
Miss Pippi le Poop
and I am
The Poop Fairy!

I heard you are
getting big and
I want to help you
learn to poop
in the potty and
then you will become
a Super Pooper!

I will tell you the story of a very happy little poop named Swimmer.

Swimmer got his name because he loves to swim in the water.

He did not like
bumping into a
diaper or pull-up.

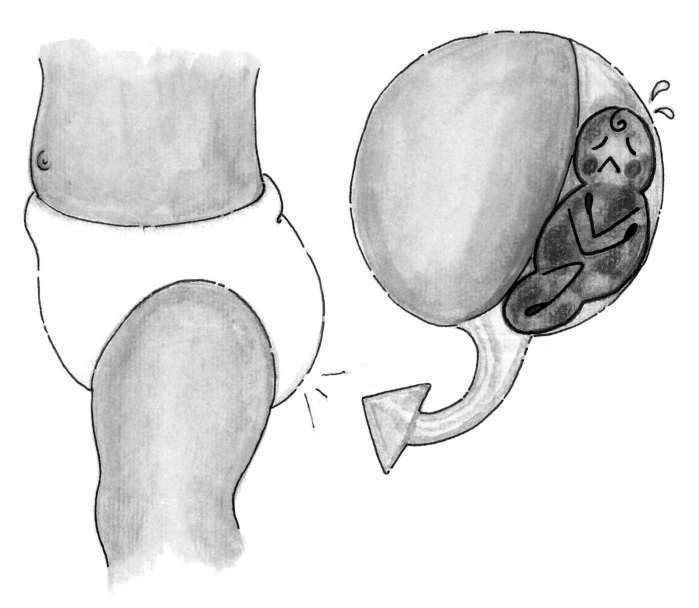

Swimmer wanted
to have a magical
poop adventure.

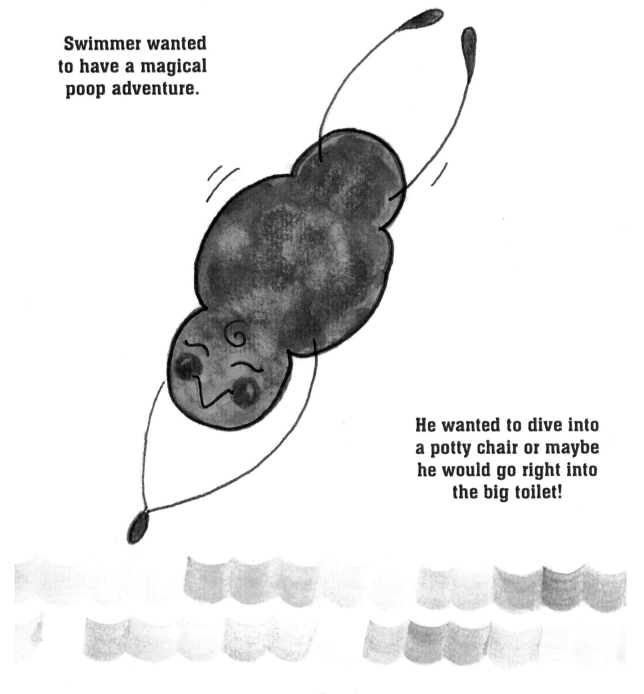

He wanted to dive into
a potty chair or maybe
he would go right into
the big toilet!

Swimmer and his friends were very happy because the child they came from was learning to poop on the potty!

11

Swimmer and his friends liked it in the water.

They had fun when the toilet was flushed and they got to go around and around and around. Next, they disappeared down the toilet and went to play at a water park.

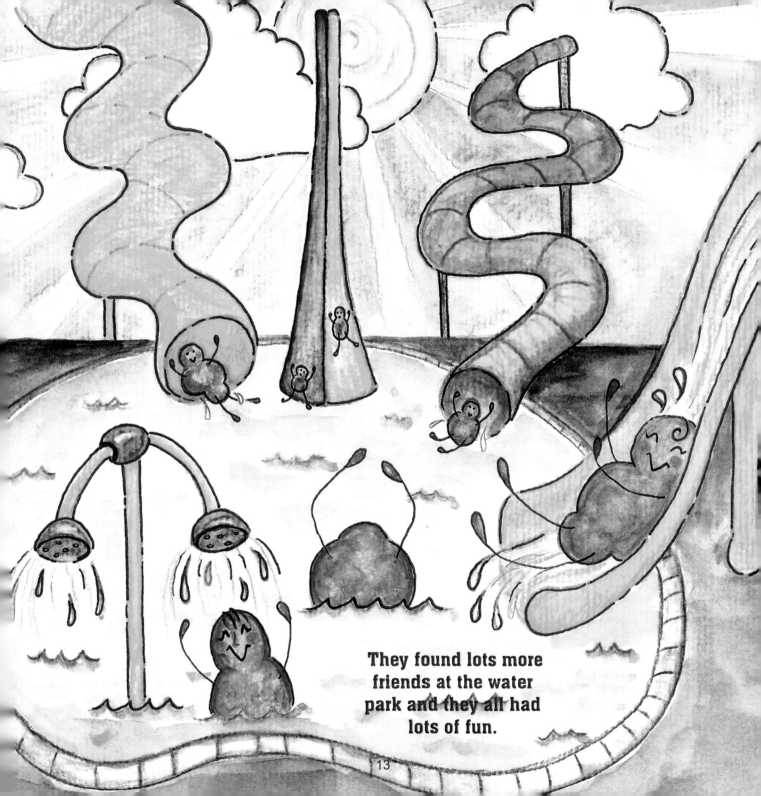

They found lots more friends at the water park and they all had lots of fun.

13

They laughed and danced and sang silly songs.
Then they went

surfing!

Soon, a very nice whale swam up and said, "Jump on my back and I will take you to meet my friend, The Poop Fairy!"

16

The Poop Fairy was very excited to meet all of the poop!

She waved her
magic wand and
turned the poop
into prizes.

18

If you want to get prizes from the Poop Fairy all you have to do is poop in the potty, not in your pants.

She will deliver the prizes to all the boys and girls
who poop in the potty.

THE END

Pippi's Pointer's for Parents
(The Poop Fairy Method)

The Poop Fairy Method will work best after potty training is well underway and your child is successfully urinating in the toilet.

Decide ahead of time on what prizes you want to use for your child. You know what motivates your child.

Expect to use rewards for a few weeks and then perhaps one final special prize when your child has mastered this new skill.

Try to avoid using food as a reward.

Make sure to keep prizes hidden from your child until they are earned.

You can have a special place that the Poop Fairy will leave the reward or have some fun letting your child search for it.

Remember, accidents happen and it is best not to make a big deal about them.

You can be as simple or as creative as you choose. Here are a few ideas of mine you can try if you choose:

- Buy a 25 piece puzzle and have the Poop Fairy leave a piece each time the child is successful. When the puzzle is complete give child a more substantial gift.

- The Poop Fairy could leave a little piggy bank after the first success and then coins each time until the piggy bank is full and then let the child buy something they want with the money.

- It could be a different surprise every time. This is my favorite!

Have fun and good luck with your Super Pooper in training!

For further information please visit Poopfairy.com